How to Teach a Slug to Read

by

Susan Pearson

illustrated by

David Slonim

SCHOLASTIC INC.

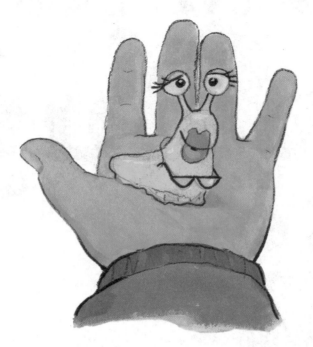

ISBN 978-0-545-51771-3

Text copyright © 2011 by Susan Pearson.
Illustrations copyright © 2011 by David Slonim.
All rights reserved. Published by Scholastic Inc.,
557 Broadway, New York, NY 10012,
by arrangement with Amazon Children's Publishing.
SCHOLASTIC and associated logos are trademarks
and/or registered trademarks of Scholastic Inc.

12 11 10 9 8 7 6 5 4 3 2   12 13 14 15 16 17/0

Printed in the U.S.A.   40

First Scholastic printing, September 2012

The illustrations are rendered in acrylic and charcoal on illustration board.
Book design by Anahid Hamparian
Editor: Margery Cuyler

When you teach a slug to read, you should:
1. Start out by putting labels on his favorite things.

carrot

worm

2. Next, find a really good book. This is very important or your slug will lose interest. The best books will have some slugs in them.

Mother Slug rhymes are good. They have *lots* of slugs in them, and the rhymes will help your slug remember the words.

ttle slug,
smooth as silk,
him in a satin shirt,
bread and milk.

3. Prop the book up close to the ground.

4. **Find a rock for your slug to sit on so he can see the page better. Be patient. It will take your slug some time to climb up on the rock.**

Mary had a little slug,
His skin was smooth as silk,
She dressed him in a satin shirt,
And fed him bread and milk.

5. Show your slug the words that repeat a lot. This will help him spot them right away.

Once a bug bug bug
on a rug rug rug

Bug!

6. Help your slug sound out words.

sl-uh-uh-g! Hey, I can read SLUG!

7. Make a vocabulary list. Slugs love new words.

Little Miss Muffet
Sat on a tuffet
Eating her curds and whey.
Along came a slug
Who gave her a hug
And told her to have a nice day.

What's curds and whey?

Cottage cheese.

No kidding!

8. **Let your slug underline his favorite words in slug slime.**

Sweet Sammy Slug
Slides through the town
Upstairs and downstairs
In his nightgown

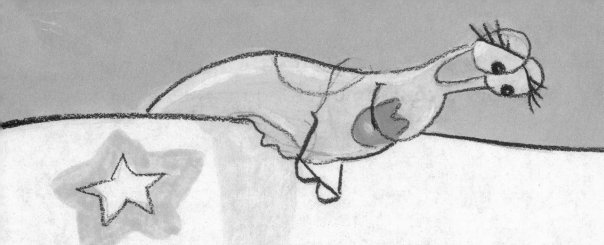

To make sure that children
Are tucked in their beds
And dreams of slug fairies
Dance in their heads.

9. Read your slug's favorite poems with him as many times as he wants. Read him other books too!

The POKY LITTLE SLUG

SLUG for President

Slug and Snail Are Friends

10. Be patient. Reading isn't learned in a day. It can take months. But don't give up— it's worth it in the end.

coated bugs And made him king of all wild slugs

And then, one day, he will read books to you!

It was a dark and stormy night!

Then he will read books to the beetles and the butterflies and the grasshoppers and the crickets and the bumblebees and the dragonflies. He may start a story hour or even a school.

Once upon a slime
when all were sleeping
a slug came creeping

Books will teach him how to play slug soccer.

Books will show him slugs in other lands.

Books will show him the whole wide world.

And all because YOU taught your slug to read!